Alaska

et

Kenai
Peninsula

Captain's Log - Day 283
rew getting restless. Still
earching for land. Lookout
otted large vessel with hundreds
people on deck waving and smiling.
disappeared in the fog. Cannot
firm report.

Gulf of Alaska

This book is dedicated to the explorers of the sea.
Without their courage and sense of adventure,
the world would be a much flatter place.

Book Design and Production
Art & International Productions
Jim Tilly and Sasha Sagan

Published by:
Misty Mountain Publishing
P.O. Box 773042
Eagle River, Alaska 99577

First Printing, May 1994
Printed in Hong Kong

Library of Congress
Catalog Card Number:
94-76042

ISBN 0-9635083-5-0

HAL'S MAGICAL CRUISE

Written by Jim Tilly • Illustrations by Sasha Sagan

Published by Misty Mountain Publishing  Eagle River, Alaska

The days were pretty quiet at the BAR King Dog Ranch until the morning the postman arrived.

"Got a letter from my family today," said Eddie. "Looks like they want to send me to Alaska."

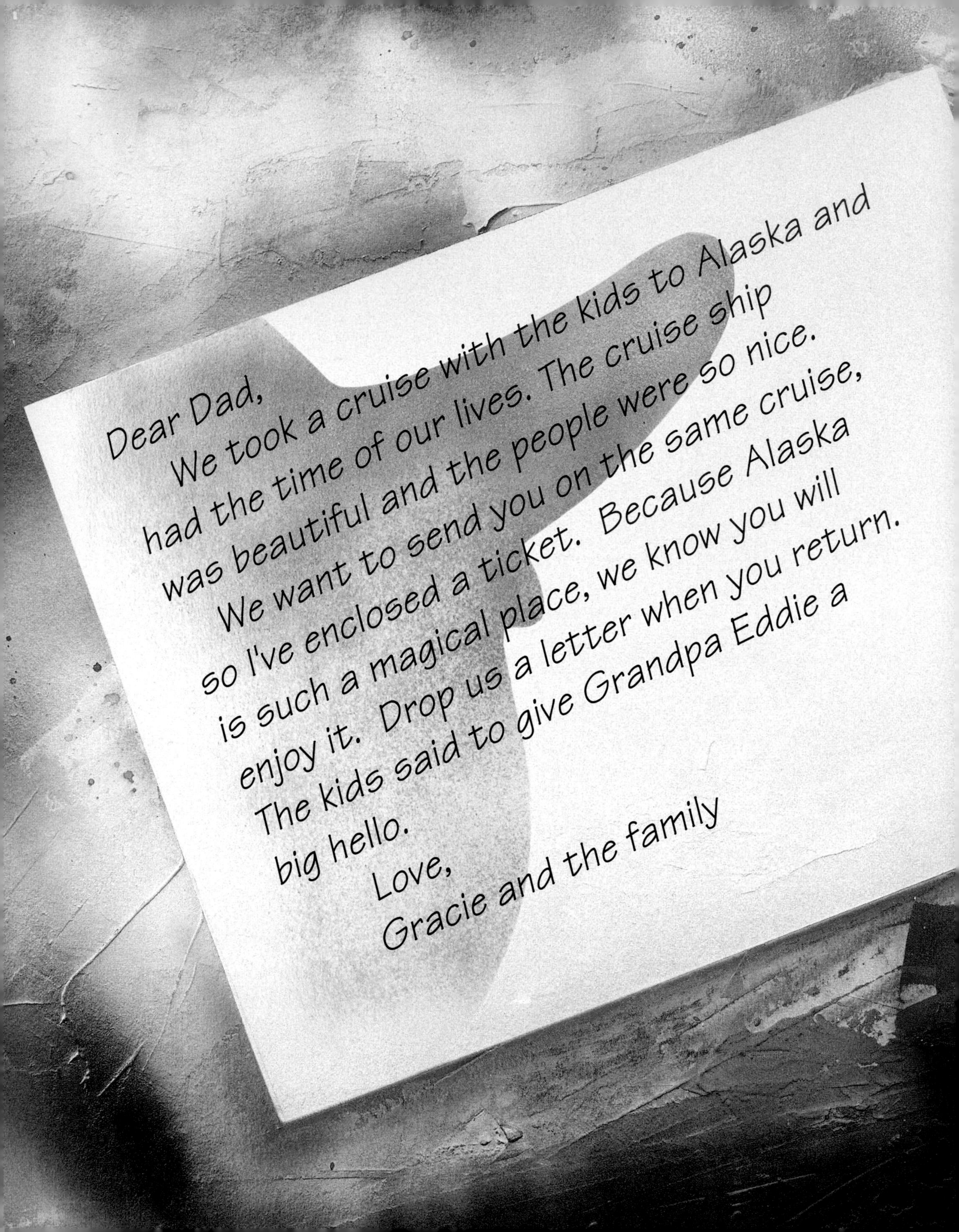

Dear Dad,

We took a cruise with the kids to Alaska and had the time of our lives. The cruise ship was beautiful and the people were so nice.

We want to send you on the same cruise, so I've enclosed a ticket. Because Alaska is such a magical place, we know you will enjoy it. Drop us a letter when you return. The kids said to give Grandpa Eddie a big hello.

Love,

Gracie and the family

"I don't know," said Eddie. "I've never been on a boat before."

"Sounds like a great trip to me," said Billy. "It will be an adventure. You've got to go."

"I suppose you're right," said Eddie. "But Alaska? It's pretty wild up there. What if I run across a polar bear or get stuck in a snow storm? And isn't it always dark? I won't see a thing."

"Eddie, your grandkids survived Alaska, you can too. Plus you'll be on a cruise ship. And I'll bet they don't let polar bears on those cruise ships without a ticket."

"All right. I'll go. I wonder what the boat will be like?" said Eddie as he drifted off into a daydream.

The next morning, Eddie pulled out his old suitcase. He wasn't sure how to pack for Alaska. He found a parka, dusty and wrinkled from years of storage, and stuffed it into his suitcase along with a wool hat and gloves. He had to laugh when he thought about actually wearing them.

He cranked up his old truck, "*Lightning*", waved good-bye to Billy and started down the long, dusty road to the airport.

Hours later, his plane arrived in Vancouver, Canada. On the taxi ride from the airport, Eddie marveled at the glass tower buildings and the magnificent mountains behind them.

The taxi pulled up in front of the pier, and Eddie began his search for the ship that would take him to Alaska. He stopped in front of an enormous boat that seemed to stretch on forever.

"Come on, Eddie. Hop on board!"

"What?" said Eddie, spinning around. "Who said that?"

"I did," smiled the big boat. "You can call me HAL."

"A boat that talks!" said Eddie. "I guess I've been in the desert too long!"

When all the passengers were on board, the boat named HAL pulled out to sea.

"Do you feel it, Eddie?" asked HAL. "Take a deep breath. Smell that clean, fresh salt air. I sure love this part of the world. People come from all over to visit Alaska. And they never go home the same. There's a special magic. I don't know if it's the animals, the scenery, or the boat ride. Whatever it is, smiles are easy to come by on this trip."

Eddie was already smiling so much his cheeks hurt.

After a restful night, Eddie left his cabin to enjoy an early breakfast. As he arrived on deck, Ketchikan was coming into view. "Our first stop in Alaska. Can't wait!" he said to himself. When the ship docked, he walked along the boardwalk and talked with all the friendly people. He followed a path out of town and into the quiet rain forest. The trees were dripping with moss and the ground was covered with a soft, spongy carpet. Eddie was bouncing along, looking up at the towering trees when he nearly tripped over a beaver in a shop apron.

"You're a beaver!" said Eddie in amazement.

"That's right, partner!" chuckled the beaver. "I'm Big Teeth Carve-a-Lot, Master Beaver Totem Pole Carver. How do you like my poles?"

"They're beautiful," said Eddie. "I've done some whittling before, but nothing like this. How do you do it?"

"See, first I must find the right tree," said Carve-a-Lot flashing his sharp, white teeth. "Then I cut it. Then chip it. Then I chop it. Then I nick it and clip it. I chew it and split it. Then I shape it and trim it. I carve it and slice it. Groove it and smooth it. Then I sand it and stand it. That's it."

That explanation made Eddie's head spin. Then the beaver gave him a special gift - a toothpick carved with the faces of the beaver's 13 children. Eddie was speechless. He shook the beaver's hand and stumbled up the trail to the large, majestic totem poles carved by the Indians.

He came to a creek with a sign "Fish Creek Market - Spawning Sale Today." The water was churning and swirling. There were thousands of fish in there.

He found a pair of goggles beside the creek, put them on, and stuck his head in the water. He couldn't believe all the fish shopping.

Back on the ship, heading for Juneau, Eddie was still excited by what he had seen.

"HAL, you wouldn't believe it. A beaver with big teeth chewing trees and making poles! And his kids were all over the toothpicks! And the fish! A big sale! Purses with fish lips! With mirrors and dresses..." Eddie was talking so fast that HAL knew he would have to wait until later to get the whole story.

Eddie finally calmed down as HAL was nearing Juneau. "Let me call my friend the Great Bald Eagle," said HAL. A blast from his horn, and soon the sun was blocked by an eagle nearly as large as a car.

"Hello, Eddie!" said the eagle. "Jump on. I'd like to show you a little of our state." Eddie climbed on the bird's back and they soared into the clouds. Up ahead, he could see Juneau stretching out in front of a steep range of mountains.

"There's our state capital, Juneau," said the eagle. "And look! It's the governor's home. Juneau has only about 30,000 people, but it includes more land than any city in North America - over 3,000 square miles! As large as this city is, you can't drive to it. No roads into Juneau! You can only get there by plane or boat - and, of course, eagle."

Eddie and the eagle flew over Juneau. Past the old mines and the steep boardwalks. Past the harbor with hundreds of small fishing boats and under the Douglas Bridge. When Eddie looked up, he was nose-to-ice with the biggest ice cube he had ever seen - the towering face of Mendenhall Glacier. The deep blue ridges sent a shiver through Eddie's old heat-baked desert bones.

The eagle glided in for a landing. Eddie slid off his back and onto the glacier. Through his boots, he felt a chill that made his knees shake and his teeth chatter. There was something very old and very cold about this chunk of ice. "This is a memory for those hot days back home," he told himself.

The eagle flew Eddie back to Juneau where he sat in the sun until his bones stopped shaking. Then Eddie went shopping and bought a hat for Billy. He heard HAL's horn blow and ran for the boat. He didn't want to miss the next stop - Glacier Bay.

As HAL slid through the floating icebergs of Glacier Bay, Eddie felt he had been taken back millions of years, to a time when ice covered much of the Earth. Huge frozen walls, like mountains in the sea, towered above them. Seals floated by on small pieces of ice.

A seal drifting near the boat yelled to Eddie, "Trade you my scarf for that good-looking cowboy hat!"

Eddie smiled and shook his head. He could never trade his favorite hat. But the thought of the seal in Glacier Bay wearing a cowboy hat made him chuckle.

When the ship left Glacier Bay, Eddie sat thinking about all he had seen. "How can I ever describe this to Billy?" he wondered.

After dinner, HAL said, " I would like to show you a part of Alaska most people never see. Look for a map under your mattress. You're in for a wonderful surprise."

Eddie found the map and followed the directions deep into the inner chambers of the ship. At a small door, he used a key taped to the map. The door opened to a room with a large, round window and an old leather chair. Eddie's mouth fell open. He dropped into the chair and stared out the window for hours and hours.

Eddie was still enjoying the underwater show when the boat docked in Sitka.

He had never seen a place of such natural beauty. The volcano, Mt. Edgecumbe, rose out of the water amidst the small islands that stretched as far as he could see.

"Sitka-by-the-Sea was the Russian capital, before America bought Alaska from Russia," said HAL.

Eddie walked around town, past the old Russian church that sat in the middle of the street. A brown bear in a fur hat, gave him a big Welcome-to-Sitka bear hug. Then he invited Eddie to meet his Russian friends and have some tea. They all sat around a table drinking the tasty tea and asking Eddie questions about his life in the desert.

Later, Eddie watched from the boat as Sitka disappeared in the distance. "I don't want it to end, HAL," said Eddie. "I didn't expect Alaska to be like this. I don't want to go to sleep, because I'm afraid I'll miss something. A whale. Or an eagle. Or a glacier. And speaking of sleep, doesn't it ever get dark here? I haven't seen the stars since I arrived!

"And I thought I had seen it all, but I looked at an Alaska map last night and my journey was just a taste. This place is huge! And HAL! What a great ride! And the wonderful food..."

HAL smiled. He would miss Eddie, but he knew Alaska had worked its special magic. "He'll be back," HAL thought to himself.

Back home again, Eddie parked his old dusty pick up. It sputtered and coughed and was finally silent. He got out, stretched, and climbed the hill to where Billy was sitting.

"Nice to have you back, Eddie," said Billy. "How was the trip?"

"Billy, it was the trip of a lifetime! I never dreamed Alaska could be so beautiful, or filled with so many amazing things," said Eddie.

"And what about the polar bears?" asked Billy.

Eddie smiled and said, "It looks like the polar bears live further north."

"Was it magical?" asked Billy.

"Well, let me see. I rode on a talking boat named HAL, met a beaver who carved totem poles, flew on the back of a giant bald eagle, and had tea with a Russian bear. So I guess you could say it was magical!" smiled Eddie.

"Well, in that case, next time I better go with you!" said Billy.

Jim (left) and Sasha live in Anchorage and are partners in Art & International Productions, a graphic design company.

N
W
E
S
Bering Sea
Aleutian Chain
Brig
Pacific Ocea